GOOD SPORTS USE TEAMWORK

By BREANN RUMSCH
Illustrated by MIKE PETRIK
Music by MARK MALLMAN

CANTATA LEARNING

WWW.CANTATALEARNING.COM

CANTATA
LEARNING

Published by Cantata Learning
1710 Roe Crest Drive
North Mankato, MN 56003
www.cantatalearning.com

Library of Congress Cataloging-in-Publication Data

Names: Rumsch, BreAnn, 1981– author. | Petrik, Mike, illustrator. | Mallman, Mark, musician.
Title: Good sports use teamwork / by BreAnn Rumsch ; illustrated by Mike Petrik ; music by Mark Mallman.
Description: North Mankato, Minnesota : Cantata Learning, [2019] | Series: Good Sports | Audience: Ages: 5-7. | Audience: Grades: K to Grade 3. | "This text is set to the tune of "Oh du lieber Augustin" / "The More We Get Together""--T.p. verso. | Includes bibliographical references.
Identifiers: LCCN 2018053375 (print) | LCCN 2018056789 (ebook) | ISBN 9781684104178 (eBook) | ISBN 9781684104024 (hardcover) | ISBN 9781684104291 (paperback)
Subjects: LCSH: Sportsmanship--Juvenile literature. | Teamwork (Sports)--Juvenile literature.
Classification: LCC GV706.3 (ebook) | LCC GV706.3 .R86 2019 (print) | DDC 175--dc23

Book design and art direction: Tim Palin Creative
Editorial direction: Kellie M. Hultgren
Music direction: Elizabeth Draper
Music arranged and produced by Mark Mallman

This text is set to the tune of "Oh du lieber Augustin" / "The More We Get Together."

Printed in the United States 6002

TIPS TO SUPPORT LITERACY AT HOME

WHY READING AND SINGING WITH YOUR CHILD IS SO IMPORTANT

Daily reading with your child leads to increased academic achievement. Music and songs, specifically rhyming songs, are a fun and easy way to build early literacy and language development. Music skills correlate significantly with both phonological awareness and reading development. Singing helps build vocabulary and speech development. And reading and appreciating music together is a wonderful way to strengthen your relationship.

READ AND SING EVERY DAY!

TIPS FOR USING CANTATA LEARNING BOOKS AND SONGS DURING YOUR DAILY STORY TIME

1. As you sing and read, point out the different words on the page that rhyme. Suggest other words that rhyme.
2. Memorize simple rhymes such as Itsy Bitsy Spider and sing them together. This encourages comprehension skills and early literacy skills.
3. Use the questions in the back of each book to guide your singing and storytelling.
4. Read the included sheet music with your child while you listen to the song. How do the music notes correlate to the words of the song?
5. Sing along on the go and at home. Access music by scanning the QR code on each Cantata book. You can also stream or download the music for free to your computer, smartphone, or mobile device.

Devoting time to daily reading shows that you are available for your child. Together, you are building language, literacy, and listening skills.

Have fun reading and singing!

What does **teamwork** look like? It means learning and **following** the rules. It means taking turns and giving everyone a chance to play. It means **cheering** for your pals and helping them when they need it. When a team works **together**, everyone can learn more and have fun.

When you use teamwork, you are being a good sport. To see what happens when soccer players use teamwork, turn the page and sing along!

COACH
11
14
6
8
3

When we work together,
we all do much better.

When we use good teamwork,
every player has fun!

Rules teach us how to play
and stay safe on game day.

Following the rules means
we are being good sports.

COACH

When we work together,
we all do much better.

When we use good teamwork,
every player has fun!

14
7
2
3

Players learn different **roles**.
We pass balls and make **goals**.

Taking turns on our team
means we all get to help.

When we work together,
we all do much better.

When we use good teamwork,
every player has fun!

We meet on game day.
We get ready to play.

Each player helps the others
and lifts up our team.

COACH
7
8
2
17
14
6

When we work together,
we all do much better.

When we use good teamwork,
every player has fun!

We help each other.
We cheer for one another.

We will do our best
and be **proud** of our team.

Oh, when we work together,
it's so fun to play sports!

SONG LYRICS
Good Sports Use Teamwork

When we work together,
we all do much better.
When we use good teamwork,
every player has fun!

Rules teach us how to play
and stay safe on game day.
Following the rules means
we are being good sports.

When we work together,
we all do much better.
When we use good teamwork,
every player has fun!

Players learn different roles.
We pass balls and make goals.
Taking turns on our team
means we all get to help.

When we work together,
we all do much better.
When we use good teamwork,
every player has fun!
We meet on game day.
We get ready to play.
Each player helps the others
and lifts up our team.

When we work together,
we all do much better.
When we use good teamwork,
every player has fun!

We help each other.
We cheer for one another.
We will do our best
and be proud of our team.

Oh, when we work together,
it's so fun to play sports!

Good Sports Use Teamwork

Pop
Mark Mallman

Chorus

Verse 2
Players learn different roles.
We pass balls and make goals.
Taking turns on our team
means we all get to help.

Chorus

Verse 3
We meet on game day.
We get ready to play.
Each player helps the others
and lifts up our team.

Chorus

Verse 4
We help each other.
We cheer for one another.
We will do our best
and be proud of our team.

GLOSSARY

cheering—shouting happily

following—going along with

goals—getting the ball into the right place on the field to get points

proud—happy about something you have done well

roles—jobs people do when working together

teamwork—working together with other people on the same thing

together—with each other

CRITICAL THINKING QUESTIONS

1. Teamwork is important for team sports. Do you think it could also be helpful at school? Tell about a time when you worked together with others. What would happen if someone didn't do their part?
2. The story talks about learning the rules of the game. It also shows kids wearing safety equipment, such as shin guards. Why do you think rules and safety are important?
3. What did the team members do to improve their soccer skills? How did using teamwork help them to improve?

To Learn More

Arrow, Emily. *Making It Happen*. North Mankato, MN: Cantata Learning, 2020.

Gordon, John, and Lauren Gallagher. *The Hard Hat for Kids*. Hoboken, NJ: Wiley, 2018.

Hammelef, Danielle S. *First Source to Soccer: Rules, Equipment, and Key Playing Tips*. North Mankato, MN: Capstone, 2018.

Manushkin, Fran. *Pedro's Big Goal*. North Mankato, MN: Picture Window Books, 2017.

Rumsch, BreAnn. *Good Sports Play Fair*. North Mankato, MN: Cantata Learning, 2020.